dear FUTURE LAWYER

An Intimate Survival Guide For The Minority Female Law Student

Guide & Journal

Neena Speer

Edited by: Jasmine Spratt

Table of Contents

Acknowledgments

I would like to acknowledge God for everything I have and everything I am.

To my late father, Donnie Speer whose mere existence made the determination I wrote about in this book possible. If you knew his story between the struggles and obstacles he faced many times and persisted through, you'd be inspired too.

To my mother, Rajesh Speer, who reminds me every day that things will work out. You believe in me to your very core and always have, and that belief gives me strength to push forward despite the obstacles.

To my sister, who saw me overcoming giant obstacles at an early age. Thank you for never letting me think less of my skills and talents, and being my best critic. You make me a better sister and person every day.

To my favorite law school professor, Montré Carodine, you breathed life into me when I was beginning to give up on myself in law school. You pushed me to keep trying and fighting!

Lastly, thank you to all my family and friends who empowered me as often as they could. Thank you for visiting me and checking in whenever you could. I am grateful and thankful for your years of faith and encouragement.

Introduction

T his book is meant to help guide law students on a path to greatness. However, most times greatness comes with a caveat: you must experience failure first. I can only tell you what I know. I made low grades, and no one prepared me for it. My personal life was so stressful while I tried to make it through law school. In my determination to succeed in school, I neglected sleeping and eating properly and avoided social activities to make more time to study. With all my efforts to succeed, I was at a loss for how little I was improving over time. My law school offered a class to help students write better. I enrolled in the course determined to get better. I remember feeling ashamed that I was going to this "special class" in addition to my other classes, but I did find a community in this class. I looked around and remembered thinking, "I am not alone." Even though this class helped us find solidarity in each other, I still felt defeated because I remember how my grades were about to keep me from my dream of becoming a lawyer. I was so ashamed that I needed help, that I had come all this way only to fail myself and my friends and family who believed in me would hear about it. I felt alone, disconnected from my classmates and friends. I was afraid to confide in anyone lest all the fear and shame I was keeping bottled up inside me come rushing from my lips the moment I opened them to greet a passing stranger. Not excelling in my law school courses almost broke my spirit. Ever since I was a little girl, I wanted to be a criminal defense lawyer, and I felt as if I had betrayed myself by failing now. I was so close to giving up that I would find myself hovering the cursor over the school's withdrawal button online at times, convinced that continuing was futile.

I can laugh lightly about how difficult law school was now, but at the time, I felt joyless and lost. I had very few friends who actually understood why it was so hard for me. I was crying and calling on my higher power nightly until, one day, I met a professor who told me that I was a brilliant young woman and that my writing had great potential. That professor pushed me inside and outside of the classroom to write and be committed to my writing. After feeling lost for so long, I found a goal I wanted to pursue. I pushed myself to do well in her class, wanting to prove to myself that I had the talent in me that she saw. By the end of my 1L year, I had the highest grade of my combined semesters in her class.

If ever there were a light at the end of the tunnel of darkness – that was it. In my success, I realized that previously, I had lost faith in myself, but with the right amount of push and support, I could do it. And that sentiment is what I want to pass on to others. For those who feel overburdened and alone, I want you to know that no matter what your circumstances are or how far behind you are – YOU CAN DO IT. This book is designed to tell you how to do it with grace, humility, and a whole lot of faith. Most of all, it will tell you where true happiness comes from in law school.

In life, we need people to tell their stories with authenticity and honesty because the truth is the most powerful story. So I promise to tell you my truth, and I hope you will feel motivated to tell your truth in the journal pages that follow. Thank you for reading my story. - N.S.

Preface

Dear Future Lawyer Letter

have been told many times that I should write down all of
my thoughts because they may help someone. So here is the
story:

At 12-years-old, as I was riding to school with my mom,
I saw a bus across the street from my school picking up kids my
age. I asked my mom why they were riding a bus to school and
we were riding in a car. I soon learned that students who live
even across the street from a "good school" could be zoned in
a way where they had to go to schools with lower funding. I
remember thinking as a child how terrible that was. I could not
verbalize anger much at that age, but I was outraged. Tell a child
to color within the lines and more than likely he or she will color
outside. Tell a child that school systems draw lines on who can

attend their school, and they will wonder why they cannot have friends who live outside the lines?

After that, I began asking the underlying reason behind the rules I heard. In high school, I finally gained clarity on why rules were so difficult for me to comprehend. Rules are not typically created to be broken. The person making the rule doesn't usually intend for the rule to be broken. Sometimes, however, the rules have to be broken because they aren't good rules. When rules are broken, we break the understanding we once knew for a new way of thinking that challenges us for the better. I honestly never thought rules would be similar to expectations for one's self in law school. My rules were to hit it out of the park with every class I took. It was not until I fell flat on my face, that I learned how to get up with grace. The wisdom that comes from making a mistake is a lot more useful than the little we learn when things always work out. When I was younger, things did not always work out in my extra-curricular activities. I was not able to be the leader in school clubs, athletic teams, and other "cliques." So, I decided that I wanted to add value to people's lives in high school. One day, I fell knee-deep into working with children at a local YMCA. I could have gone many paths with this discovered passion for helping others, a social worker, a police officer, or even a waitress. However, I knew that becoming a lawyer would impact the kids I served by helping them chase their bigger passions as well. At first, I was a program participant, but soon I became a volunteer. Who knew that I would be there for the next nine years? After college, all I had as work experience were YMCA internships and the YMCA camp counselor jobs that I held for six years.

When I finished undergrad I knew I would miss my friends and wondered what law school would be like. When I finally was accepted into law school, I wondered how my classmates would be often. I met my law school classmates during our summer Contracts I class. I really enjoyed having a pre law school family before I came to the infamous 1L orientation. It was nice to have people who I went through this with beforehand. In a class of 30 people, I may have easily missed the different personalities, but I did not take it for granted. My biggest success was learning every one of my classmates' names and something special that they brought to the class.

As you read further, you'll see the different types of students and stages you'll likely encounter throughout your years of law school. There will be people in your classes who have the characteristics I described and you will think you have them pegged. There are so many more people that I did not include like: the party goer, the extreme sports buff, the loner, the job bragger, the grade bragger, the internship bragger, the social media updater, the fun one who has a serious side, the library kid, the ambassador, the dream killer and more. However, my purpose in writing this book is to share guidance. I cannot prepare you for every person you could imagine, but this book will give you information that will help you transition, observe, and prepare for a successful law school career.

I want you to read and figure out what makes these people special and what makes the overall law school experience unforgettable. What makes these people and their perspectives stand out in the classroom in their own special way is both their perspectives and them. Each add unique value to your class.

The best advice I can give you in law school is: do not join a clique. When I say a clique, I am not referring to that group of friends that band together with you in the library or that group that loves to serve others in the community. What I mean by cliques is to join people who would prefer to treat law school like it is still high school, who talk down to others, make you feel like the dumbest person in the room just for being different, and those who have not fully grasped what it means to be "a good lawyer." This means you are also a decent, kind human being as well. I urge you to be your own person. Make your standards firm. Stand by who you are and value every person even the negative ones. Those are the people you are going to owe for a lot of your success.

P.S. Dear Future Lawyer, I was just like you. Scared, confused, doubtful and unconfident in my own ability, but my secret was I relied on God. I was at church every time I could go. I went twice a week second semester. I cried a lot. I took a lot of personal days. I did not get the top grades, but I did make lasting friendships and gain positions that helped me give back, and I thoroughly enjoyed my journey to becoming a lawyer. I cried in a lot of teachers' offices, prayed in tears, and cried in bathrooms.

However, I lived for God more than I ever had before. I grew stronger spiritually than I ever knew possible. You are going to face many battles when you get to law school but just know that this is not just my story. This is the story most of your classmates won't tell you because they want you to think they have it all together. Let's be honest. They don't. We don't. I don't. But I survived and graduated, and now, I can share my journey in hopes that you are encouraged to continue your pursuit of success and happiness. Trust the Process. Trust that it all works together for your good!

Signed,

Neena R. Speer, Esq.

— A girl who dreamed about two careers, a Lawyer or a WNBA player, and somehow ended up in law school. That schedule I give you is real. These tears & these hard times happened. But with Jesus, I survived and thrived. Thankful.

What It is Really Like

<u>Let me tell you a story:</u>

A young girl enters a swimming pool. She climbs down the ladder slowly, trying to adjust to the cold water. She pauses as her feet touch the floor in the shallow end and anxiously glances around, seeing small groups of friends playing in different areas of the pool. She decided today would be the day—the day she swam to the deep end. She hesitantly steps forward, deeper into the pool. She takes a deep breath and steps forward again, feeling calmer and reassured. As she lifts her foot a third time, someone suddenly splashes her. The girl looks over to see someone, smiling and giggling, who splashes her again. She moves away from the splasher, towards the ladder, rethinking this decision to reach the deep end today. As she puts her hand on the ladder to leave, she takes another deep breath and decides not to give up. She turns back towards the open water and barely registers the next splash of water to her face before it hits. She hears more giggling as she wipes her face, squeezing her eyes tightly shut at the sting of the water. Upon opening her eyes, she sees a different person before her. The splasher giggles and asks, "What's taking you so long? Do you...." She looks around as she lowers her voice to a whisper, "...not know how to swim?" Before the young girl can answer, the splasher giggles again and swims away, their feet kicking vigorously, splashing more water onto her. Though confused, she decides not to give up trying to swim and starts to step forward again towards the deep end. Splasher 1 calls to her from the other side of the pool saying, "What kind of swimsuit is that? You look so unattractive in it." Splasher 2 snickers and swims up to her friend. They glance at each other, smiling, and turn away from the girl. The girl feels embarrassed, her face flushes, and she ducks under the water, holding her breath to calm down. The cool water embraces her skin as she imagines herself home, relaxing, far away from all of this. She bursts up from the water feeling more confident. However, just as she begins to step forward again, the two splashers swim up to her, watching in silence. She glances at them, and they giggle again. The young girl steps forward despite their harassment. They laugh again. She steps forward again. They follow her, smirking at each other at her attempts to swim. The young girl steps forward again, only to fall forward, her face dipping into the water. She reached a deeper part of the pool without realizing it. The room echoes with the sound of laughter from the two onlookers, yet the splashers do not move forward from the shallow end this time. The young girl begins to tread water as she moves farther into the deep end. She glances back at the splashers, still lurking in the shallow end, but no longer laughing. With renewed confidence, she plunges to the bottom of the pool and kicks off from the ground. She shoots forward, her arms and feet moving to their own rhythm as she sails towards the deepest part of the pool. She turns onto her back and floats on the water, smiling to herself, triumphant.

Law school feels much like that, Future Lawyer. It won't come easy. Most days, it's going to suck. However, the swim from the shallow end to the depth of your potential and talent is far more rewarding than the empty success of titles, plaques and awards. To graduate from law school is to overcome adversity in your spirit. No amount of studying will prepare you for class exams or the infamous bar exam. You will always feel like you do not know enough. However, remember there is a reassurance that will come to you while taking the exam that will confirm that this is the path for you. You will have a mini victory when someone tells you that they look up to you, they believe in you, or they are proud of you, and that will make the brunt of difficulty you face all the more worth it.

The Plunge

Dear Future 1L

I write to you today to recount a reality often experienced but very underestimated and a tale often embellished. If I can give you any riveting advice it would be: don't answer the phone while driving unless you think it may be a law school acceptance call, then YOU MUST definitely pull over and answer the phone. For the call, you'll need three things: a laptop/notepad, a seat, and food and drink. Don't call back until you have all three. You are about to embark on a journey that people dream about, and you don't have the stamina to take that news lightly.

You know all that jive about there being two important days in your life. #ScratchThat. Every single day is the most important. But the day you are accepted into law school, your life is on the landing strip towards extreme alterations approaching fast. So first, let's see how you classify.

Pre-Law School Cold-Feet: The day you are about to start 1L Orientation, you have found fifteen reasons you are going to fail, no one is going to like you, and you are thinking that you must have been crazy when you clicked submit. (Don't worry we all go through this one, sometimes during the school year and sometimes all year long.)

Law School Rookie: It's your first day. You only have one fear: the infamous "cold call." You read the case, briefed it, and now you must wait. The minute hand begins ticking faster. The professor has not even arrived, but you just know today is DOOMSDAY. You really hope the variation of highlighter colors in your book are enough to show you tried. Your professor just arrived! Now your heart is beating fast. "What is this damn case about? Maybe I should lead with a joke? What if I just say I don't know? Maybe this professor will leave me alone." Class is over. Saved by the bell. Dang, what was class about? (Don't worry everyone goes through this, and YES even the gunners!)

Gunners: I got this class. I have analyzed large quantities of data before, so this should be no problem. I'm going to raise my hand because I know I have the right answer. I think the professor may be confused on how to read the Rule against Perpetuities. I figured out how to explain it to the whole class. (Keep in mind no law school student has ever been able to fully explain this rule). The way I see it, this is how the law is supposed to read. Do you want my two cents on fairness or logic behind the law? Well, I'm going to offer it anyway. It's hard being the only one in class who gets it. Nobody else raises their hand with such confidence. Did the professor just ignore my hand? I must not have raised my hand in time for it to register. I will try again. Class ends. Boy, I tell you raising your hand all class is hard work. Dang, what was class about? (Don't worry, there is always one who makes an attempt to know every answer. It is only a phase most times, but sometimes it is just who a person is. Don't let that deter you.)

Jokester: If everyone laughs at my jokes, they must like me. You should try to make a joke in every class that is self-deprecating. Get people to laugh at me. Then surprise them with my amazing wisdom. I laugh a lot because life has been difficult, but I do not see class as serious as everyone makes it. I cannot come to class knowing everything. I sure am going to try my best though. Most times, it sounds like I'm joking so people laugh. However, I'm usually seriously confused. (Don't worry laughing is the best medicine for class. Don't lose that spirit, sometimes law school is serious and we need to be focused, but most times we all want some comic relief amidst these long pages of block quotes and law texts. Without your laughs, law school can feel overwhelming at times. Trust me you'll need it – especially on those hard days. In time, you'll get it.)

Spaced Out Cadet: *Cold call* spaced out Cadet: "Yes, I just think if you read the case this way, you can find that the parties were fighting over this as well." Professor: "Where are you reading that?" Spaced Out Cadet: "I'm not sure exactly." (Don't worry, that student just made it so much easier for you to understand because now the teacher knows that someone is lost so all of you are probably lost and not saying anything. Thank you, Spaced out Cadet!)

The Quiet One: I'm really not trying to get called on. In fact, I am not going to raise my hand. Let me write down the important points in class and ask questions only when I am confused. I also need to schedule meetings with my professors. I am trying to figure out which day works best for one-on-one meetings. I wonder if this class will end up being a class I like or one that I have to mentally prepare for every day. Do I care if my classmates think I'm an idiot? A little but not really. I have 15 other things to worry about. Like my family, how I'm going to get food all week, should I start a budget, what classes should I take my 2L year? (Don't worry, if this is you, chances are your professors like you, and your classmates spend all of their time trying to make sure you get your "cold call." You will do just fine and maybe find out that it's better to be quiet most times in law school.)

Now that we've classified you, I know what you really want to know about is the array of emotions you are about to experience. The INFAMOUS schedule awaits!

Law School One Week In: I think I got the hang of this case brief thing. Let's try to outline so I can be ahead for exams. Noooo, there's a bar review. I HAVE to go to that. I mean, right? It's the first week. I cannot be too serious right now. I won't make any friends! Wow, there is a bar tab for free drinks? Law school is awesome! I need to go to more of these. Wait, there are like twenty people here that I know. The rest are upperclassmen! Man, I knew I should have outlined! I am a terrible student. I'm going to fail. (Don't worry you're not going to fail, relax!)

Law School One Month In: One month down, nine to go. No scratch that, we are going to count by semester. One month down, four to go. Wait, did our teacher's just assign us 300 pages for tonight? What happened to the one to three cases a night. Wait, why am I in law school? When do we get a school holiday? Is it Friday, yet? Wait, why in the hell do the upperclassmen have no Friday classes? This cannot be fair. They always chilling. Maybe I should be chilling. I want to go out and have a good time. But, I guess they earned it. I should, too. (Don't worry you can still go out, just remember eventually you might want to start outlining-- Never mind, go out have some fun!)

Law School Two Months In: Everybody keeps going out to party every week, like when do they study? I cannot hang, or maybe I can? We still have like two months before exams. I heard there is a costume party for Halloween. I HAVE to go to that one. But I probably should be outlining and practicing. Football season is heating up! There is a football watch party tonight! Man, why am I in law school again? I'm tired. Why are all of my friends traveling without me? Do we get a Spring Break in law school? Wait, it's still fall! (Don't worry, this is what everyone likes to call mid-semester crisis. You will get through it.)

Law School Three Months In: I have now accrued enough knowledge and note-taking to formulate this foreign object known as an "OUTLINE." What is it? How does it work? How can I use it to annihilate my law school exams? Upperclassmen, please show me your ways. I should probably join a study group. Well, I guess it's a little late for that or is it? Man, this outlining thing is hard. There's a lot of information. I should have been doing parts of this as I went along. Man, it's been five hours and I am still outlining Torts. Today is just Torts day, I guess. When am I going to read for these classes? Should I just stop reading? What if I've been doing it wrong this whole time? I'm dropping out man. No, I cannot do that. I'm already in debt. And they said I can't work. How will I sustain myself? Why am I in law school again? Exams are in one month! I'm going to fail! (Don't worry, at this point, it is normal to freak out. Go to your happy place (i.e. church, park, restaurant, outside,

Starbucks, etc.) and chill. It's not as bad as you think. Call a good friend for help!)

Law School Four Months In: Today is absolutely the most difficult day of my life. I am about to take my first big exam tomorrow. I don't feel ready. I haven't prayed enough. I have cried too much from total exhaustion. I really know nothing. I feel like this semester was wasted. I don't even have a great outline. I thought I would be more prepared than this. All of my friends probably hate me because I complain so much. I have no one I can call for encouragement. I should probably be studying. No, I need to sleep. I guess I have to give it my best shot. When they call time, I HAVE to be done. I don't want to fail. I really don't. (Don't worry you will not fail. Look at it this way. You made it four months longer than most. You have the stamina to keep going. You are just running up a steep hill right now, but every hill eventually goes down. It gets easier.)

Law School after fall exams are over: I never thought happiness felt like a full box of donuts, a glass of wine, or a drive back home. Oh man. I have missed so much. Time to update social media. #OneSemesterDown. Christmas has to be amazing this year. I need family time. Surround me with love. Wait, why is school starting back so early? January what? I need until like the end of the month at least! (Don't worry if your winter break goes by quickly. Get back in gear right after New Year's. Grades are coming! Batten down the forts and batten down the need to share information like what you thought of the exam, how you think grades will fall, and your job prospects.)

Law School Spring Semester: Who wants a job? Do you have a resume? Attending the job fair this semester? With all of this, you still want me to take classes?! When are semester grades coming out? Should I be wearing a suit to class? Why is she wearing a suit, does she have an interview? Wait, I need to focus on class. Why are all the professors acting like we are going to be depressed when grades come out? I probably failed, but then again I could have passed. The world may never know until the end of January. Oh my, not the rat race, again! (Don't worry once you get grades things do not get any easier. It is best to start this semester with a blank slate than to wait for grades.)

Law School Five Months In: I just finished being exhausted from last semester. Is it just me, or did the classes get so much harder? Did they just give us 300 pages to review on the first day? What happened to easy transitions? What is so wrong with having syllabus day? You know those days in undergrad where we got mad because we didn't do anything. Yeah, I want those days back. Thank you for the school holidays. Lord, please be a snow storm! I don't want to go to class on Monday, Tuesday, Wednesday or Thursday! Give me a Friday! Is this semester going by faster? Wait, I'm not ready to take exams again. Oh shit, grades just dropped. Time to go look. *Shuts computer and locks self in room, doesn't come out for two days.* (Don't worry some people have very good grades first semester, that is why there is a top 10% in the class. However, just in case you are not one of those 13 people, you are still amazing and grades cannot define you. Work smart this semester and pick yourself up.)

Law School Six Months In: Still recovering from grades. Still feel like a failure. Oh, how nice it feels to be done and not fail. I wish my grades in undergrad could transfer so I could feel remotely well about my GPA. Why is this so hard? I need help. I'm getting a tutor. No, wait you have to pay a tutor. Maybe an upperclassman will have pity on me. Wait, why are we writing a brief? I'm not doing law school work over spring break.

I deserve a break! This is a full week off from law school. I am not doing work. I promise. Well, maybe I will do a little. Ok, I am going to get ahead. I haven't slept in seven days straight trying to crank out this brief. What is wrong with me? Why can't I relax? What has law school done to me? Why am I even here? I'm going to quit. I could get a good job right now just for trying law school. Oh crap, I got a call-back for a job interview. Now, I have to stay in school. (Don't worry so much about grades that you cannot change, focus on the job you just got lined up for the summer, that new executive board position you have, or that journal you are going to write on this summer.)

Law School Seven Months In: What the heck is going on? How do we have exams again? I just got back from spring break. We turned in the brief, but man I failed that! I killed that oral argument though. I can do this lawyer stuff… I think. I HAVE to study early this time. I am going to have great outlines, ask for help, and get in a study group. I will do so much better this year. *Cries for the next two weeks thinking about all the studying.* I plan to ask for help from everyone. Teach me this class again oh wise friend who's an upperclassman. I will make it. I'm tired. Why am I doing this to myself again? It is election time, should I run for something? Nah, I'm tired. However, it may help me to get a job later. You know what, what the heck. I'll run for two things, maybe three. Just when I began to doubt myself, I received a call telling me "I got the job!" This law school thing is starting to grow on me. (Don't worry, you will do just fine, and you have the 2Ls and 3Ls around. Please do not forget to ask for help. It is all around you. You are not alone.)

Law School Eight Months In: The only thing we have to fear is fear itself. I only have one more exam at this point. I am highly considering dropping out because this semester was so freaking difficult. After this last exam, I can say it. I just have to cry it out until then. I am so unprepared. Perhaps even more unprepared than last semester. I have no idea what I am doing, but I refuse to fail, give up or drop my head. I have to take this last exam. (Don't worry we all feel like a failure after most exams. You ever notice how many people group up after the exam to talk about what they put down and look at you wide eyed like their soul has died a little? Trust me, you did better than you think. If for some reason you did not do well, go meet with your professor and find out why in the fall. Don't forget over the summer.)

Law School after Spring Exams are Over: I'm done. Keep the pencil. #FirstYearDown. I'm no longer accepting calls, emails and texts concerning law school for at least two weeks. Goes ghost. (Don't worry, taking this trip is not gonna set you back. I took a trip to see my best friend graduate after I finished the next morning. I flew out at 5am to another state to be far away from all things law school. You will need a break. Take it.)

Summer Job after 1L Year: You're either paid or unpaid. Clerking for a judge or interning for an office. Answering calls or doing legal research and writing. Training, brown bag lunches, and daily legal jargon. Assignments, drafts, revisions, and more drafts. Your job is never done. Are they going to feed us? Do we get fancy badges? Will I love this job for the rest of my life? Do I hate it? Will they like me? Will I like them? I'm just going to come with an open mind. Wow, this summer taught me a lot about working in this field. Boy, it's a rat race. Morning traffic, 5 o' clock traffic and sleep. All of these are important. This is about more than just the title. Forget LinkedIn likes, do I like me? Is this where I see myself? Who am I? Did I make a journal? Am I going to try out for a competition team? What else am I going to do to give back? Wow, I'm low-key excited for school. But shhhh, don't tell my classmates. I am silently celebrating but crying on the inside. (Don't worry, by this point you should be a bit excited for school because you made it through a huge emotional roller coaster and they did not kick you out. Summer jobs definitely help you figure out what you do not want to do, so make sure you get your hands in every opportunity you can to grow. Only one more summer before graduation, bar exam, life.)

If you're like me, you're either experiencing one of three emotions after reading all of this: (1) this girl has a lot of time on her hands, (2) how does she know, or (3) how is this going to help me?

Allow my experience to inspire you and give you hope to keep going even when you feel like giving up – you will survive, just like I did.

Best Regards,

Neena R. Speer, Esq.

— A 1L Girl who had to hit rock bottom because she was on top of the pack at Howard, but she needed a lil humbling to get to her next level...

My Law Student Journey 1L

The Journal for #DearFutureLawyer

By: _____

If I could describe my feelings 1L year…

This is the journal where I share my thoughts about my law school experience… I promise to write everything in here as raw and real as possible. I promise to let this be my sacred place to vent about what I am truly facing in law school. Sometimes, I tell even my closest friends I am okay even though I am not. So here is where I will be honest with myself.

Write to me about your 1L Year…

_____
_____
_____
_____
_____
_____
_____
_____
_____
_____
_____
_____
_____
_____
_____
_____
_____
_____
_____
_____

Thank God I don't look like what I've been through! Don't take your little victories for granted.

Did you accomplish something that is better than when you first started?

_____
_____
_____
_____
_____
_____
_____
_____
_____
_____
_____

I'm so thankful for this 1L Year Victory/Loss because…

_____
_____
_____
_____
_____
_____
_____
_____
_____
_____

The Rat Race

Dear Future 2L

So, you're still here, huh? Law school didn't scare you away? I mean that is the premise of what 1L year is all about, right? Wrong! It's your last chance to walk away before you feel obligated to stay and finish it out. You see, there is a process that happens over the 1L summer that produces this spirit of resilience within you or an "I'm done with the BS mentality." I like to call it "remember your dreams before this" stage. It occurs suddenly and unexpectedly, and many dedicated and hard-working people realize that law school is awesome in parts, but accepting the challenge of finishing is sometimes overwhelming.

Your 2L year is very different. You encounter different obstacles. In 1L year, there was help everywhere, and there were people all around you to help you get through the hard times.

However, unless you were fortunate to have someone who was willing to sit down and teach you how to do each thing from 1L year, you are just as lost. You might even be more lost than 1L year. Now you are forced to be selfless and help the students coming behind you when most times you are struggling to help yourself. 1L orientation is here again – because let's face it, the world moves on. You had your chance to have a pity party. Now, it's time to forge forward and excel at being a 2L even though you still feel like a 1L, just with a new title.

Common Experiences:

2L year is like being handed a stack of papers and told to run with it. No direction, no assurances, just the benefit of knowing you are not a 1L anymore. What does that really mean? When you were a 1L, people checked in on you and asked you how you were doing, offered you outlines, gave you words of encouragement, etc. That kept you on track, but now all that help and guidance and loving support is gone. You have to do it on your own. You quickly realize that you preferred 1L year when you had this comradery of students all going through the same issues at the same time. Now, you picked your own classes, so it's not like you can just call your friends up and create a study group. Now you might actually have to talk to people, including upperclassmen who may not be as helpful this round. You don't see the competitiveness until 2L year. However, in most schools, you will find upperclassmen willing to help you with your struggles if you look long enough.

Competitive Experiences:

Let me adjust that for those who did not have that experience. You don't see the competitiveness until 2L year if you are fortunate enough to go to law school that does not have students who rip out pages of textbooks in the library because they think that removing a critical case or body of law from you will somehow give them the advantage. However, in the age of information, young future lawyer, "everything is online now," so their efforts are fruitless most times. If you are at one of those schools, well my advice to you is to develop a tough inner fortitude because otherwise, the disappointment that comes will eat you alive. Let's veer off here for a second. It is important to address the "over-competitiveness" at some schools. It does exist and there are schools that are like that. Where they are, I could not tell you. However, you will notice an elitist personality on how the representatives sell you on attending the school. I am in no way condoning this behavior by these schools, in fact, if you do choose to go there, I think it is imperative that you point this behavior out to the administration and work on eradicating these practices. Sometimes, it feels like you are the only one fighting that school's culture, but it can change when you have the courage to combat it. Now one option is to not go there at all, so always keep that in mind, but you will miss the opportunity to impact this culture for the better.

On the other hand, if you do choose to go to a school like that, please do not go easy on them. Force them to help you, and find allies quickly to ensure you are talking to the right people at the right times. If all else fails, don't quit. At these types of schools, the only way to change them is to survive and succeed despite them. Then, you can tell your story when your position is more protected. Unfortunately, at these schools, institutional shaming works best. You have to make them feel bad for not being more helpful. Most of the time, it is because of "sticking with what they have always done" and "who they have always hired." It is not until people are forced to deal with the more trying and difficult decisions that they learn to be more open. I am in no way recommending you slander your school, but if you ask for help and demand them to be accountable and they fail you consistently, then speak your truth.

Who to Study: If you read any book about law school, they may tell you how to study. They may even tell you what to study, but they will never tell you who to study. Study the top 10%, the 13 people in your class, because what they do for success is going to give you better insight into the infrastructure of how law school works. If you see these people cramming for every single exam and never going out to any social functions, then you are looking at the exception to the group. Most of these people are at some parties, have bigger financial awards packages, or may have a parent who donates large amounts of money to the school. These students are also the school's top mascot or brand ambassador, and they will never say anything adverse about the school. These people have behaviors, study groups, journals, allies, and activities that enable them to do well. Sometimes, your high performance is based on emulating good techniques you have observed from other successful people.

Grass Isn't Always Greener on the 2L Side: Sometimes when you are 2L, your rosy glasses are forced off, and you see that you are going to have to make some serious adjustments to survive either in your technique or your surrounding environments. If you are able to accept that and be excellent despite where you fall on the curve, then you are far ahead of the rest. However, if not, then you realize how you were all on the same playing field up until your 2L year. As soon as it hits you that you are in a class with 3Ls, you begin to see the true drawbacks of the curve. Hopefully, there is a 3L who took your class their 2L year that takes pity on you and help you make it through. However, keep in mind, it will be difficult most days, but you will get the hang of it. Trust me.

Law School Is A Lot Like High School At Times: On top of the school work, there is a system set to recognize one form of success. See, when you come to law school, they recognize that you are brilliant and awesome. I mean that's why they accept you and offer you a seat. What they don't tell you is that there is "a way" of doing things and that if you don't learn to follow, you will sometimes fail to see aid or assistance. Law school can feel petty, mean-spirited, and messy sometimes. You will find yourself asking, "Why do people gossip so much about EVERYTHING?" They gossip about grades, about their most hated professors, their most coveted clerkships, who flunked, who dropped out, and all the while you are just trying to stay afloat. No one sends you a letter warning you that you may experience turbulence while you are here. Family members may pass away and you might still have to take the hardest final in your life the next day. You may be going through a hard time because you lack the social skills to be "accepted" by your classmates. Maybe you don't go to enough bar reviews, or maybe they do not like you. Your classmates might be the messiest bunch in the whole wide world, full of gunners and braggarts that just make those monthly bar reviews all about them and their accomplishments.

Fortunately, just like high school, you will meet some people that make you so happy you chose to go there. You will find some friends that make coming every day worth it. Those people will get your weird and understand your craziness. These are the friends that you don't have to discuss grades with because every time you get together, you all laugh so hard your bellies hurts. Hold out for those people because I kid you not, we all hated high school. We all remember the popular kids, the loners, the smarties, and more. Well, they all exist in law school too. The difference is they are just a new level of intelligent and a new level of competitive, spiteful, and sometimes just mean. Some folks may make you cry. I cried because of a few people when I was in law school, but those great friends I told you about make it so much better. Just make a point to find those people even if they aren't law school students. You need those people future 2L for all the hurdles that lie ahead.

The Politics of Your Law School GPA: Anonymity feels like a figment of your imagination. Grades are so important here. They are the single most important source of access in different spaces in the building. You can see students with high GPAs at the heads of journals, competitive teams, ambassador programs, and even speaking opportunities for the school. If you have high grades, the doors that are open are held wide open. The issue lies in your people skills that go with the grades. I can honestly say that the people who have both people skills and high GPAs in law school see very many doors open. Now, I want you to know, that I never had a high GPA, so there are ways to open doors for yourself wherever you fall on the spectrum. Now, let's be honest, it is a hustle. They always say this at the very beginning, and we falsely nod pretending to understand we know what this "hustle requires of us." We don't, you don't, and I didn't.

The hustle is so different for everyone. I have advised countless underclassmen on some steps I took to open doors in law school, and some could easily pass through, and some had more difficulty. I would venture to say that opportunities to be a shining star at law school are wrapped up in your GPA, your networking prowess, and your ability to know your purpose and operate in it strategically there. My purpose in law school was taking my writing to the next level, and by my third year, I was published in a reputable law journal. You have to figure out what your end goal is at the school. We all want to leave a legacy, but we don't know how. My skill was speaking, and I was fortunate enough to network with the right person who put me on her conference slate two years in a row. My law school was made aware of my success, and I ended up on the school page for my talent not once, but twice. The second time, I was even able to bring some of my classmates with me.

Leaving an impact is about doing way more than just making the grades or receiving the accolades. This is about pulling someone up who comes behind you. If you go through law school only driven by your success and your GPA, you will find that though you may find a way to still win, it will feel empty when you reach the apex of your journey: graduation. You may want to represent the school, you may be doing amazing things in the community, and you may be making an impact in an extracurricular organization – but it means little if you have not figured out a way to parallel your interests to what the law school's interests are. Most students want to know how to find success in law school. For me, success is simple. Follow rules or break them, your choice. Each one has its own strategy. Sometimes, you must bend for administration. Sometimes, you have to hire a tutor. Sometimes, you will have to be silent about your struggles. Regardless of it all, you will find success when you remember to pay it forward for any opportunity you receive.

The Politics of Burnout and Fatigue: There will be times when you have to pretend like your world isn't falling apart. Many people suffer depression during law school, but no one talks about it. Often times, we struggle alone. We cry in our rooms at night because crying in someone's office signals weakness and a need for counseling. Why? Because everyone, including law schools, are not fully equipped to deal with their students on a personal level. There is a nice, sanitized law professor-student relationship that is the norm for most students. The issue I have found is that when a law student shows emotions of any kind, even normal human frustration, sadness, or financial worries, they might be seen as unstable. However, I challenge that thought with the belief that each student just needs a safe space to vent, cry, yell, or be silent for a minute. The most that seems to come of these situations are "I'm sorry this is happening to you," "We will get someone to help you," or "You should really talk to the school counselor."

This method of dealing with students is a bit difficult to process for a student who feels like the best people who can provide encouragement and a safe space don't know what to say when their students come to them with problems other than the class material. Some students encounter professors who make them cry, professors who make arbitrary rules, or tenured professors who cannot be fired but have harmful interpersonal techniques. This type of behavior is normalized in law schools, not just for students, but for professors, for professionals, and law firms as well. This is a reality that you must strategically counteract with a plan so that you avoid being disappointed in people. This may mean that you focus on the positive professors and faculty and continue to sing their praises to administration or it could mean that you begin speaking up against these professors who harm you with a responsive safe space within the law school to address grievances.

The Politics of Making Strategic Allies in Law School: In politics and in life, there are always allies who will help you, but you will have to seek them out. Those same allies need your praise sent to the top administrators so that the school hiring committee can become more open to the new hires that present these characteristics. They need positive evaluations, critiques for the better, and support from their school. What allies do not get and often need from the school administration is a meaningful interference when intolerant, misogynistic, unaccepting, non-inclusive, elitist behavior is occurring or is reported. This does not mean fire tenured professors. It means give harmful tenured professors less oversight into their classroom rules, less class slots, and more accountability when they treat students and fellow faculty and staff members in a way that is intolerant. It may be necessary that law schools create a policy to fix these prevalent issues created that is taken seriously and all parties, including tenured professors, are held accountable. A policy that would end up working for the greater good of all of the students.

The Politics of Course Evaluations: Please understand how inaccurate a student's course evaluation can be if it is more positive for a professor than it is for another based solely on the student liking them or not. The positives should be based on the fact that the teacher made him or herself available, provided resources, and gave practice problems often. It should also be based on if students had a question that was substantive, that it was answered and that the exam review was helpful and showed where the points are that they lost. However, the positives are often based on experiences of students for a hard subject matter. That is not accurate if we take into account implicit bias that could affect students who might never see a professor in a positive light because of how they view the world and how the exam "should be."

Implicit Bias/Bias: We are given as students too much of a space to take out our micro-aggressions on a faculty member who is doing what they need to be doing. If something negative was said to us, we should be encouraged to say that before the evaluation. It is unproductive to dump out all of your negative thoughts about a person at the end of the semester just because you did not like the professor or the material. That is not ok. It is better to make evaluations the last step for productive and constructive criticism. In today's age, young adults are much more likely to write harsh things about a person in a digital space because they can dehumanize that person there, but they are not as likely to come to the person who caused the issue. That is a problem. If you find yourself frustrated, I encourage you to talk to the faculty member because chances are, they have not fully understood how you have been struggling. If they did, they may have adjusted to help you understand the material better. This is very necessary. Even a bad law school professor can greatly improve their teaching style if given an opportunity to discuss with the student in a professional manner what they struggled with in their classes. The bias that is often reflected in these evaluations can be racial, gender specific, sexual orientation, religious values, and more, but it may be time for law schools to take a real overview of these professor evaluations and have each other read what students write to other professors. I have had many conversations with teachers that were shocked to hear what some students were allowed to say in another teacher's classroom and what some professors said to students. It may be time to push the conversation for a more candid, direct discussion with the student and the professor as opposed to having a catch-all for student aggression at the end of the semester to berate staff when stress is at an all-time high because of exams and other obligations.

Allies after Law School Professors: Law school professors have a great deal of influence on your critical years during the first two years of your journey and even after that. They write recommendation letters, teach you first hand, and some can even develop into some of your very best supporters in the future. They may send you job opportunities, scholarships, published research writing opportunities, or be a mentor when you mess up in the inevitable after law school journey. The way we treat our professors matters just as much as how our professors treat us. Therefore, I would advise you to find a professor or two to make a sincere relationship within your legal career. I can't even count how many times I have reached out to my old law school professors for things I needed help with, successes I have had, and defeats I have faced. You owe it to your future to get to know these people that you write a review for and take classes from. They are a wealth of knowledge that has not even been completely tapped. Some professors will never make that connection with you no matter how hard you try. So my main and only advice is: don't force it. It will happen.

Jobs, Bar Review Courses, and More: How do I get a job? As a 2L, you are still trying to figure out why you didn't get a handbook to jobs in print form your 1L year. In fact, I am still wondering that, too. I never really thought that my entire life would be decided at a mid-point, but that's just what they ask you to do. Decide your life at a midpoint. Well, Future 2L, I think it is important for me to remind you that you are not a halfway mark. You are not a checkpoint. You are so much more. But who cares about my random affirmations and validations. You want to know about jobs, right? Well here goes, you will need something called a **legal resume**, not to be confused with that crap you used in undergrad. This is a whole new resume made for legal minds who have analyzed the greatest pieces of legal doctrine and black letter law. They do not care that you met a U.S. President or the fact that you run for fun, though that is always good to mention in an interview. It makes you different, so save that running story for your meeting **in chambers** with your loose but fitted suit on and your nervous chest palpitations. After you have obtained something called a **legal resume**, you now need a wild thing called a **cover letter. Cover letters** for legal jobs are a crude and harsh protest between you and your perceived accomplishments. So, kill the "I really want to work for you" and "I have always dreamed of doing this" lines. Instead, you need to publish this authored, meticulously combed and coiffed version of yourself. One that speaks with a cadence of flattery, demonstrated grammar proficiency, and precision. Unmitigated and supernatural precision is key. Don't worry though, career services is good with helping you be precise. Right? No, wrong. That is not your only trusted editor. You must become one with the paper in front of you. Ask yourself rather harshly, does this matter? If your impulse is to say "no" whether jokingly or not, cut it. Save yourself the derision later from a trusted editor. After, you have a working draft because this is in no way final. Do it all again. Do it so many times that your eyes are tired of looking at it. They are just over it. Then, you can finally stop. Now it's time to obtain this amazing gift from the law professors you managed to impress and ask for **letters of recommendation**. Please do not take the "no's" personally. I mean it. It is a blessing to be thankful for. You want only the people who feel they know you best to write them. If it takes a while for a professor to get back to you, just ask another one.

You will eventually develop your tribe of always on call professors and advisors who will be on standby just to write you a letter. Please do not forget to thank them with a handwritten note as a small but very sincere token of your gratitude for all the work they have done. Do it because they did not have to help you. They chose to help you in your legal career. Keep that lesson in your heart always future 2L and you will go far. **Writing samples** are the absolute worst and there is no easy way of getting around reviewing them. They are draining and time consuming. So, please dear God, take courses that force you to write a darn paper, because you will need many writing samples once it is time for job applications. It is very difficult to provide a writing sample for an unguided course, so take a "paper" class as soon as possible. Please don't try writing your own writing sample before applying for the career of your dreams. **Transcripts and other items** are not something I am going to give you a pep talk on. Get over your grades. Let the chips fall where they may. Please be ready to always pay for these requests, but there is a little secret called "Word, copy, and paste." Please do not spend a fortune buying official transcripts when you can just update a Word document with your recent marks.

Bar Review Courses: I cannot stress this enough. During 1L year, you took only bar classes. If you are at a school with a high bar passage rate, focus on taking courses you love from 1L forward. I am serious. It is like yoga. Set your intention for the rest of your legal career. If you go wild about evidence and race, then focus on that! Do not get caught up in the hype about "bar classes." Do get caught up in the hype and sell bar review courses. Why should you sell? Because you get a free bar review course. A course that costs thousands of dollars, and it is free if you push others to buy some. Please understand there is nothing out there that will guarantee you bar passage, but if you fail, it only means you were meant to tell an awesome testimony. Please do not sink into a depression, if possible. There are so many people who do not pass and are meant to show others how life works sometimes for the better. If you had passed the first time, then you could not tell a story that inspired millions. Please always keep that mindset when you fall short of your own "self-imposed expectations."

Externships instead of class?! I can do that? Please do not limit yourself to the summers to gain work experience. Look for semester programs where you can work instead of go to school. Honestly, you need to know what it's like to be out there working from 9am to 5pm. What better way to explore that than while you are still in school? If the semester program is offered in the fall of your 2L year, take it. If it is offered in the spring of your 2L year, take it. Do not wait to take it. Taking it in your 3L year is good, but at this point, you will have already become disillusioned with school and only go to party. But you need to finish as strong as you can. My best advice is to do this followed by a study abroad, and then opt to not work at a firm but work for a professor you admire and respect over the summer. By this time, you have developed closeness with at least one of your professors. Ask them for work in the summer. Focus on coming back to 3L year refreshed.

End of the 2L Summer: Your goal is simple. Figure out a way to break free from all the bad stuff in all of your years prior to this point. I mean really work on actively trying to let it go. Bad relationship? Say goodbye. Bad friends? Stop calling them or being so available. Bad school experience? Practice proper self-care. Bad personal life? Go home and visit more. If that is not good for you, then go to the place that feels like home to you. Set that as your goal. Strip yourself of all the people, places, things, and experiences, past or present that rob you of experiencing your best 3L year like nothing before. They didn't pick you for journal? Who cares! You never got to be on a competition team? Go join someone else's team. I'm serious. There are places where your skills will be appreciated within your school if you do not make the first round picks. You never got that class you wanted and now they don't offer it? Take some classes at the university that you always wanted to take. You might find that you now have special treatment to join those classes and will be treated like a brilliant legal mind. Which you truly are! I refuse to let you start your Dear Future 3L journey until you have worked on pruning your way of thinking. It is destructive to see yourself as a series of pluses and minuses on some checklist of your self-worth. You will never experience 3L year correctly if you think like that. I am so serious. Please cut off all destructive thinking. If you need to see a counselor or therapist at this point, then book an appointment or tell your most trusted objective friend, but do not carry it into your 3L year.

How Does She Know? How Does She Do That? She Can't Possibly Understand Me! She's Never Met Me!

It's okay. I would have reacted the same way. Except I have met you. I met you because I was you. I met you every single time I failed, hit my head, stubbed my toe or got doors slammed in my face in my 2L year. I met you every single time someone talked down to me, hurt me, used me, mistreated me, and screwed me over and I still had to go to class and act like everything was okay. I met you last week when you got that email that said "Sorry there were many qualified applicants, but you were not one of them" and you cried yourself to sleep. I also met you when you got the email that said "You were chosen.

Don't mess up or it might affect your employment package." All you have to do is finish, but now things are so final, you wonder if all of this was even worth it. You wonder if this job could have waited until you "felt like a lawyer." Please understand me: loud and clear. It's not worth it if you are unhappy every single day you go to class. It's not worth it if it is physically painful for you to go to class. It's not worth it if you fantasize about quitting every single day. You know what is worth it: remembering why you started. If that is not larger than why you are finishing, then quit right now. Don't look at it as a loss. It is your victory. It is you saying that law school is not worth my happiness. Please do not misunderstand me: I am telling you to quit law school right now if you are still unhappy. I mean it. I won't encourage you any more than that.

Now if you choose to stay, stay because you want to find happiness here in this new journey. Stay because the alternative is not chasing your dreams. Stay because you made a promise to yourself to be a lawyer and you are tired of running away from that. Stay because if you don't stay, you will let YOURSELF down. I do not give a crap about anyone else being let down at this point, but you. You are so important to me. I want you to have an experience of a lifetime, but you cannot do that until you have fought through your internal crossroads of: "Do I really want to do this?" My answer was, "Yes because I dreamed about this when I was a little girl. Yes, because, I found something here at law school that lit my soul on fire and exposed me to something I never even knew I could do. Yes, because being a lawyer is not the only option after law school. I can do what I enjoy for the rest of my life and never go back to this if I do not want to. Yes, because having a job is not more important than being happy to me. Yes, because if I leave now, it will not be because I am unhappy but because I am scared of chasing a dream no one believed in but those closest to me. I never thought I would be in the position to prove others wrong, and I finally realized that I cannot care about that anymore. I finally realized I have to do this for me. That scares the living crap out of me. Yes, I want to finish for me. It is finally clear that I have to dedicate this to a better "me." My past is not why anymore, and that is so scary. My past is my story. My "why" is a "me that I can be proud of." This "me" comes by facing my fears head on. Facing the fear that none of this was my dream at all but a way to contradict others. On the other hand, maybe just facing the fear that this is my destiny helped me realize it because it was the only thing I consistently fought to keep." Look future 2L, whatever you do: you must decide: YES or NO? You cannot do that until you let everything go that held you back. Let it go right now. 3L year is coming, and there is no time to take your foot off the gas.

Sincerely,

Neena R. Speer, Esq.

(a girl that made it through this 1L story, but then realized 2L year that being happy was far more important than anything else in the entire universe. Money does not measure happiness, and neither does prestige.)

My Law School Journey 2L

2L Year Be Like…

Round 2. What is for you, it is for YOU, and no one can take it from you. Live a life of which you are proud. Breaks are well needed when trying to maintain your focus, your stamina, and your overall happiness in the world.

Take some time out for yourself today and journal about how far you've come…

_____

_____

_____

_____

_____

_____

_____

_____

_____

_____

_____

_____

_____

Did you make a journal? A competition team? Did you book a class? Are you barely making it through? Are you frustrated with grades yet? Are all the high GPA students in your class this year?

Just remember, Dory said it best… "Just Keep Swimming."

_____
_____
_____
_____
_____
_____
_____
_____
_____
_____
_____
_____
_____
_____
_____
_____

HALFWAY: A J.D. CHECK POINT

Take some time out to celebrate your halfway point and the amazing adventures and opportunities you've experienced. Do you know how many people never even get to this point in their legal career? This was hard for you. I know life was thrown at you fast in the last three semesters. I would say that calls for a celebration.

So go somewhere amazing for New Year's or do something you enjoy and tell me all about it…

_____
_____
_____
_____
_____
_____
_____
_____
_____
_____
_____

2L second semester: When life kicks you twice as hard

By this point, you've had an amazing New Year's or did something that your future self will thank you for. Don't think about last year— really crack down on finishing as strong as you can this semester because I guarantee you won't regret it come 3L year.

Write to me about how you pushed yourself past your comfort zone this semester…

_____
_____
_____
_____
_____
_____
_____

The Servant

Dear Future 3L

"This little light of mine. I'm going to let it shine. This little light of mine. I'm going to let it shine. This little light of mine. I'm going to let it shine. Let it shine, let it shine, let it shine."- My Hum as I walk in the front doors for the last year but first day of the new academic year.

There is a price for breaking free of bondage, future 3L. That bondage is a hard set of chains to eliminate. See when you let go of everything, *(like I hoped you would the summer of 2L year, but you probably did not, I know I didn't)* you also let go of parts of you that have always defined you. That might have been a bad relationship you needed to end, a friendship that has served its season, or your old ways of living that kept you from being the leader that you are now. Say it with me now, YOU ARE THE LEADER. In two short years, you managed to rise to the top of the alpha pack. Now, whether you like it or not, people need your help to navigate the troubled waters. You are the only one who knows how. You are the only one who has been there. But if you are like me, you did not let it go. You carried it into 3L year, and now it is holding you back. Instead of helping people, you are dropping off the map, out of reach and leaving the school. All of this is because you have some desire to have a job your classmates will finally be proud of or that YOU can be proud of. Then, of course, everything will be good. You close yourself off and get to work on those **legal resumes, cover letters, letters of recommendation, writing samples and transcripts** which have become your life. You need money, so you apply for scholarships. You need grades so you hit your classes with a ferocity that consumes your thoughts and you APPLY, APPLY, APPLY, and APPLY. You will not be a failure to your classmates. You will get your dream job. You will have awesome news to share with your social media friends soon. News that will elicit thousands of likes all for some stupid form of validation. That's what will happen. You will seek and seek, and people will call you supernatural, amazing and blessed.

BUT

You will forget what it feels like to show common human weakness. You will forget that the long nights and early mornings eventually hit you. You will learn that after you have lost people to death, sickness, and timing that life will not wait for you to get the job or finish school. You find that you have to deal with the person that is left after the first two years of law school: yourself. You might not like anything about yourself.

You might have hated who you had to become on the road to graduation. You might hate everything about law school, but you have got to let it go. So because of this internal self-loathing, you miss opportunities to tell someone "you can do it" on a day they really needed it. You miss lunches with underclassmen that just want to be around you and know that they can do it, too. You miss being able to help someone just because you are there at school, but instead you are "trapped in your own head" with "your own problems." This is not about you anymore. Maybe when you were a scared 1L, maybe when you were a hurt and healing 2L, but now you are it. You are the only one in the whole law school, professors excluded intentionally, that can show human kindness to your fellow man that was just there two years ago, in fact 2 months ago. You are the only one who can tell them to "chill and stop talking about this law school crap and develop social skills," and they will listen. But instead you tell them "it's normal," it will pass," "find your way," and "don't worry." It's your fault when all they talk about is law school. It's your fault when they never stop getting on your nerves because you never told them how to be truly successful at this. It's your fault when you don't tell them to stop asking you about grades because it's not important. Why is it your fault? Because that is the only reason you ever talked to them in the first place. You never asked them how they were doing and so you created "super lawyer computers" who have no idea how to process their emotions properly. It's your fault because you never went out of your way to make their life easier than yours was. You only helped those who asked you, and you never did more than necessary. That is not helping. That is padding your resume future 3L, and I'm frankly sick and tired of hearing people say "it's not your job" to help them. It is so your job. It is your job to be blunt and direct with underclassmen about when to stop being crazy people about grades. It is your job to scream "stop the madness" and do crap that is inconvenient for you for once in your legal career that wasn't "all part of the process." So, I dare you to get uncomfortable this year. I dare you to help your fellow man. I dare your race to graduation competition become about who you can help next and do not keep score. I dare you to help everyone you meet in some way because honestly 3L year is crap if you do not learn the lesson of service to others. That is what you are about to be – a servant to others. So, I'm done with all the parties in your honor or the networking events to get a job. No, I'm done with anything that does not enable you to help others. Damn it, you get a spine and make that your intention this year, or I swear the legal profession is in for a negative tumultuous downfall. I don't care what it takes, make your road to graduation the bumpiest plane landing possible. If you do not start helping people now, how in the heck are you going to do it once you pass the bar?

Why is she talking to me like that? I am a great human being! She is wrong!

Am I wrong about you? Do you find people to help every day? Do you find a way to help someone in your class, another class, the world, your teachers, the staff, etc.? Do you? If not, you are failing. You are so failing. You do not deserve your degree. I frankly cannot tell you how many times I asked myself what is wrong with law school. Why do I feel so terrible some days? Because sometimes to survive, you have to develop a "forget everyone but me" mentality. And sometimes, that mentality is embedded so deeply that you find a way to tell yourself that through your new lens, you are a service to others. However, if you are upset every day and ready to leave, you are limiting your full potential. You are the reason why you fail. You are the reason why you are not at the place you want to be yet. I want you to know that you can be happy right where you are if you remember your duty to help other people, future 3L. You have to remember that it hurts sometimes to help when you are hurting, but this is not about you. Your job in life is to make someone's life easier, and you simply cannot do that if you are not helping every single person you touch in some way. Your smile, your spirit, your energy should electrify your space. You should be the battery that recharges the world. You have to commit to being "light" and not necessarily lighting the darkness all the time, but lighting others who work in jobs that they don't love just to pay the bills. You have a duty to encourage others to follow their dreams. You cannot graduate without remembering that.

This is not about the selfies, the accolades or the publications. This is about being a servant. You will be a terrible lawyer if you don't see that now. Your only mission is to make others' lives easier. I know that completely goes against the self-care articles that have been used as propaganda. I think in life, we need balance. Self-care is a way of balancing so you can go back to being this person. But you are not supposed to self-care every hour of every day. You have hard work left to do. So no, you're not going to like me for saying this, but get over yourself. Get over the fact that your boss is full of crap because he is. Get over the fact that you do not like school most days, and that is okay. But don't let that deter you from finding a place where you can help others, and they truly see you operating in your highest calling. That is the only thing I wish for your future 3L, because if you find this overarching need to help others wherever you are planted, you will see it. You will see what I have been talking about. You will make a difference in this world. I want that for you future 3L. I want that for you like you wanted an A+ your 1L year. I just want to see you happy. I am not there yet, but I am so happy with the work I am trying to do on myself and the ways I help others. Make it your intention future 3L, and watch your life change forever. Trust me. I have been there. I know.

With Highest Regards,

Neena R. Speer, Esq.

(I can finally appreciate this process of letting go and being open to greater things in my life, and I believe you should, too. Find your tribe and help the people who still need to find their purpose, their reason, and way to help others. Find happiness. It matters to YOU!)

My Law School Journey 3L

What do you hope to accomplish this last year?

Set your intention for 3L year below in the open space:

Take a moment to thank your higher power or whoever or whatever motivates you for bringing you to this moment. They are going to put your composite photo on the wall this year. I can tell you this #3LOL is what third years use to describe not caring anymore about law school. This is a concept in my book that was not my reality because I vowed to push myself to do the best and most awesome things I missed out on in my 1L year and even my 2L year. I would say #3LiveYourBestLife instead because it is really your best time. You have mastered two years' worth of hardship. You can do this. You have already come so far. Finish strong.

Write to me about the 3L battle you are facing…

_____

_____

_____

_____

_____

_____

_____

_____

_____

_____

_____

_____

_____

_____

_____

_____

_____

_____

_____

_____

_____

_____

_____

_____

_____

_____

_____

_____

2nd Semester 3L Year: Don't mentally check out yet

I know you are ready to throw the papers and tell the professors to keep the pencil after that last final you took. You're looking at next semester like, "Run me my degree!" Don't check out, yet. You can work towards publishing your final writing samples for these classes in journals. Submit your best written work this semester and expand your portfolio for your brand and your future lawyer impact. Trust that you can do anything you put your mind to.

Write to me about the best law school essay you can think to write....

_____

_____

_____

_____

_____

_____

_____

_____

_____

_____

_____

_____

_____

_____

_____

_____

_____

_____

_____

_____

_____

_____

It's the last final of law school!

Tell me how you're feeling…

_____

_____

_____

_____

_____

_____

_____

_____

_____

_____

_____

_____

_____

_____

_____

_____

_____

_____

The Grind

Dear Future Graduate

Grad

G **raduation:** This might feel like a huge accomplishment. This might even bring you to some tears, but if you are anything like me, it won't feel as good as undergrad. You are so excited to finish graduation and go on your "before the bar exam" trip that this will not touch your heart as much. Even after you graduate, all you will be thinking about, even if you have a job lined up, is the bar exam and what that pass or fail means for your future.

Bar

The Bar Exam: This exam is hard. Let me repeat that for you again. This exam is hard. You are not going to come across an exam that compares to this in law school. Your frustration and last-minute cram sessions will not help you on this exam. Dispel all of those emotions two weeks leading up to this exam prep course. I am not kidding. I mean cry, have fun, get out and live for two complete weeks before you start studying. It is not a gym workout. This is an exam that you might shit your pants studying for because it is just that hard. Now that I have scared you enough, let me walk you through the options and considerations.

Bar Prep Courses: If you were smart when you first started law school, you decided to help sell bar prep courses for a company. In return, they gave you a free course. This is almost a required purchase for any savvy law student at some point. Do not miss out on this and end up paying $1,500 or more for a bar course.

Pre-Bar Vacation: Please take a full vacation and relax. Do not think about the bar. I repeat, DO NOT THINK ABOUT THE BAR. If you spend any time thinking about the bar, please start your vacation all the way over. Now, relax and have the time of your life because your life is basically over once you return from vacation.

Starting Bar Prep: I am going to be honest. The worst part of bar prep for me was listening to others compare their study methods to one another. Don't doubt your own study habits, do what works best for you. Honestly, the best practice you can get is to start doing the MBE questions from the question bank and learn why you are getting them wrong. The lessons are a good supplement to what you are learning again, but remember that your mind will retain what you practice, not what you hear through a lecture alone. It is the same with your law school exams. You can have an amazing professor, but their lecture alone will not prepare you for this exam. My best recommendation is to head to your local library and allot time each day to study uninterrupted. Go someplace where you will not see your classmates. Also, practice questions and review answers in places where there is some noise to distract you. When you maximize your efforts in a place that is somewhat noisy, you hone a focus that conditions you for any situation that can come up on the exam. You also prepare yourself for that annoying clicking noise or that bar taker who likes to talk beforehand about how they feel. I prefer silence and seclusion on the days of the exam, but more than likely someone will be there to spread seeds of worry and doubt. Your objective is to train your mind to be un-phased by any interferences or hindrances.

This is not something you will enjoy. In fact, you may quit, slack off or fall off on studying at some point. "Do not quit" is my only advice. Do not compare your time to others. Do the work with the time you have left. I know it is hard to believe that the bar exam can be given some slack, but no one is able to stay with the study schedule or goal they set out to complete when studying. Your goal is simple: get as close to your bar exam prep goal as possible. Do not rely on computer programs or the bar exam study progress in these bar courses to let you know how much studying you have completed. Keep a personal account of your progress.

Failing the Bar Exam Worries: I always lived by the mantra "failure is not an option" until I failed the bar exam. I know you are wondering how someone who failed could possibly give you advice on how to succeed. However, please don't think that failure means that person has no quality advice. I was a victim of that mindset. Someone tried to help me once, and I shrugged off their advice like that could never be me. I was a conqueror and no bar exam would stand in my way." I was also stubborn and unreceptive to learning these concepts again to a point of mastery. When I first studied, I would know the rule like when I was a 1L but had not mastered the concept. I failed the bar exam on the first attempt, and it took a while to be able to say that with pride. That failure humbled me. It made me understand that I still had more left to learn. It helped me see that a young black Indian woman who had accomplished so much could hit a wall. I was devastated when I got the news. So I want to prepare you in case that happens to you or if you worry about it like me. You are not in charge of your destiny. I need you to hear me. There is a bigger plan in place. Please do not think I am saying that God meant for me to fail. However, I will say that in my failure, I had to stop looking at myself as the hottest new lawyer and force myself to understand that that year I would only have a JD. Remember, the bar license is a final step to becoming able to practice law as a lawyer, but it is hard to obtain and study for. You will appreciate it later when you accomplish your dream. Failure in a case, a class, or even your bar exam is an indication of a place where you have not gained a spirit of gratefulness yet. Instead, we sort of expect it to happen. When you find yourself thinking that is what you deserve after all your hard work, you will miss the point. You are a young lawyer. People do not support your career. People do not believe you are going to do the best job. People do not believe you deserve the paper your name is printed on. There are people who fought and got hit with rocks and negative and nasty words from people for you to get that license. You are doing this for a legacy you stand on: whatever that may be. You are meant to change the world, but you cannot do that with a mindset of "entitlement." Entitlement means always thinking you deserve something that you have not put the time, blood, sweat and tears in to achieve. Ask yourself when you get into this worry mode or if you fail – did I put in the time? Did I give it my all? Did I pursue this with good intentions? The answer to these questions determine a lot of your circumstances in this field. Entitlement is also believing the falsehood that working hard for something means you are guaranteed to get it. If you have trouble with these thoughts, I want you to gut check yourself quick. What is necessary for you to pass will vary based on each individual's story and specific obstacles. What matters is if you pursued it and tried. Even if we fall short of the pass the times we take the bar, the fact that you fell and keep getting up says volumes about your character. Don't forget that.

Breaking Down Bar Prep Strategies: Before you get started, you need to ask yourself these three questions: Am I ready to commit the study time to prepare for this? Do I have an accountability partner or encourager? Why am doing this? It may seem natural to take this exam fresh off the graduation stage, but this is something that takes time, stamina, and discipline.

"One who lacks discipline lacks productivity" is something insisted upon by my father. He always told me that the key to anything is self-discipline. I did not fully understand how true that was until I tried to study for the bar a second time. For me, in undergrad, I could get the same top grades with minimum effort. I realized very early on as a child that I never really had to learn anything, just memorize. I can do that exceptionally well. I even won a prize for memorizing eighty names in my Harvard Business School Summer Venture in Management Program (SVMP). The cool thing is that there were only 81 of us, and we had less than a week to learn this. I thought I could wow my law professors with this same skill of being able to memorize large amounts of law and regurgitate it on an exam. Well, I soon learned that while it is clear that I knew what the law was, my explanation was not superior to that of my classmates. I was floored. I had used this skill to impress countless teachers in most classes since I was in elementary school. My classes were hard but once I really committed to memorizing the lesson, I could take the exam with ease. However, law school ended up being like my Linear Algebra class where I decided to help someone else do their homework instead of studying hard for my exam because, frankly, I knew math. I soon learned from my professor what a "D" really looked like. I asked her how I could make sure I received an "A" in her course because I did not want to have a low grade. She imparted to me that I should study hard for every exam and that my focus needs to be on my classes and not on other people's classes. I studied hard, and I even had to secure a tutor. By the end, I had received an "A" on every exam after that one. My end grade turned out to be a "B." The lesson I learned is that discipline with my studies would quickly have eliminated ever getting that grade, but I did not truly have discipline until I sought out help and applied myself. So what does this have to do with the bar exam? I am explaining that memorization alone is not going to work, you may need a tutor, and also do not try to be "captain save everybody while studying for this exam.

Memorization: I bet you have been good at memorizing in school, too. This exam does have some degree of memorization in it. However, if you think you are going to memorize every possible law that the bar examiners could possibly throw at you, you are wrong. You are in for a rude awakening. That is 14 subjects with over 50 pages of law text per subject. If you would like to memorize all of this law, I will not stand in your way. I will not tell you it is impossible. However, I will tell you that it is counterproductive if you have not mastered the concepts in the text. I will tell you that strict memorization gets you good points, but well-reasoned legal analysis must be demonstrated. Memorization does not present that opportunity as often as practicing and getting answers wrong. When you are critiqued about your analysis or even your rule statement, it helps you remember how to state the law. When I used Kaplan, the graders did that for each submitted essay. I may have completed over 20 essays, but I became skilled at getting answers wrong so I could learn how to say the law the correct way. That is a much better approach to large bodies of law.

Tutors: Some bar prep courses offer tutoring services. I have not used those because I found a tutor locally, but regardless, these tutors realize that there is an established pattern to what is tested, how practice questions should be done each day, and how you should structure your time and your writing. If you are not very knowledgeable about the exam or you do not study well in large groups of people, find a tutor. If you have no experienced lawyers in your family and cannot creatively study for exams, find a tutor. If you just want to pass the exam, find a tutor. It is worth the investment. A tutor is an accountability partner. A tutor is a physical person as opposed to a lecturer on a screen. A tutor can give insights into strategies that will work and that have worked on this exam. I highly recommend getting a tutor in addition to your bar prep course. It helps way more than you know.

Put Your Oxygen Mask On First: There are some things that come up in our lives that cannot be helped. For example, a loved one could get sick or require care. However, outside of your family and close friends' suffering and needing your help, you need to prioritize helping yourself. I am not saying that you ignore your friends, but I am saying become less available and less responsive. You have to take this exam seriously, and it has an adverse effect on your body, your mind and your spirit if you are still trying to maintain your nights out with the girls or guys weekly and study. Give yourself a schedule, pack a lunch, and do not let up until you have crossed the finish line. I am sure you have friends and mentees that need your advice and words of encouragement. However, sometimes you are going to need the encouragement. You need to surround yourself with people who understand that and will support you.

Do Have Fun: Lastly, when you first start, you will see fun happening out in the world. Please do not hibernate completely. Please go out for dinner or give yourself a treat on the weekend as motivation. This is a study practice you want to complete. If you have to move in with your folks or support system for that time. Do it. Please do not alienate yourself from the people who provide love during this time. You will need them when you get really frustrated. Trust me. Also, please get some sleep. It does nothing for you to drive your health into the ground as a sacrificial lamb for this one exam. You need sleep. Listen to no one who tells you otherwise, and get at least six to seven hours each night whenever possible. Sleep renews the mind.

When You Pass the Bar: I hope you ugly cry, fall out, and praise your God up and down. I hope you do not call a soul or answer the phone or post on social media. This is something that you had to work for and have faith in the result coming back in your favor. You deserve your own celebration. When you take the acknowledgment of your accomplishment, take it with a sense of gratitude that reaches the depth of your heart. I know you are proud, but let the world humble brag for you. I want you to stay focused. This is not a time for you to throw a party and put the world on your back. This is the time where you learn the depths of this profession. You find a person willing to mentor and grow your talents. This is not the time to show off. I know your friends are going to brag about this, but you accomplished a next step towards the future career in your journey. You need to remind yourself that an "Esq." is not an excuse to forget your lessons so far. You are fighting a system that is broken and needs help. You can either become a hall of famer or a pretender. I want you to succeed. So please walk across your swearing- in ceremony with humility and great reverence for all the sacrifices that got you here. Then, get to work. I want you to know that "life after passing feels like preparing for the bar exam." You will be working on becoming sharp and staying informed for the rest of your career.

Lawyer

How to Find Happiness after This Wild, Wild Ride: I know you have made it through everything that a young attorney has to encounter. However, the most important thing after law school is happiness. Somewhere after all of your job searches, billable hours, expense accounts, networking events and happy hours, we all want to find happiness. It is not elusive. It is simply the answer to this question: Did I do the right things for the right reasons in every area of my life? If you answer no somewhere, you still have time to fix it. The answer to this question turns on what you define as "right." Right can mean fairness or things that balance the scale. I am sorry to inform you, but the scale will never be balanced fully. In order for the scale to balance, you would also have to have a direct hand in the actions of other non-compliant persons standing in your way. This often comes up when you view this profession as a sword for battling good and evil. The best phrase I learned in law school was "it depends." It depends is so powerful because it helps us understand that there are always many different ways to view a set of facts. The structured boxes in your mind of good and evil must fall away in the practice of law. "Right reasons" depends on your motive and intent behind what you do. Do you serve yourself and promote yourself selfishly without trying to help others understand how to follow in your footsteps? "Right things" depends on what your actions are when no one else is watching, snapping a photo for the "gram" or recording video footage for a good deed versus just doing the work.

I want you to be happy because I firmly believe it is within your reach. If my father, who has been disabled, an amputee, and in and out of the hospital can find the joy in his pain and hardship, I know anyone can do it. If I can fail a bar exam on my first try and still inspire a young person to not quit when the door slams in their face, I know you can do it. You can do amazing things, but you have to check your motives and the timing of your well-intended actions. When the world can be truly touched by who you are, then you have tapped into your purpose. Your purpose is based on what you do from your heart.

Have a young child watch you for a day or bring your friend's child with you to see how you live. Children are not fooled by what society overvalues. If that child looks up to you, ask yourself every day if you would behave the same way if that child was watching. I have learned that children humble us better than our peers, because we are more mindful of the bad habits that we possess when we are with them. If you are ever in doubt about the type of person you are, learn to see yourself through the eyes of children. They will help strip that "famous persona" that "superstar mindset" away from you. The reason why is because that child was once you. You had a hero that inspired you once, and made you want to do the right things. Don't ever lose the child in you, and when in doubt remember how a mini you would see you.

Final Words: You can still have the job you want or the future you want. It is all possible because you are not in control. You are standing on the shoulders of those who did not get to have this opportunity. Your only mission in life should be to leave the world a little better than you found it. You can do this by helping someone up, giving guidance, and being transparent to those who look up to you. Your happiness is within reach regardless of where you end up after law school. I want you to know that law school sucks. But I also want you to know that pursuing law is a journey that changes your life. I hated law school most days, but I am happy that I had the opportunity to go and succeed. Now, I see so many people follow in my footsteps, and that warms my heart. One day, there will be more minority attorneys, like you and me. That is the most exciting part to me sometimes. I wrote this book to let you know: You're not crazy. These people are mean and cold sometimes, but I made it through with my positive spirit intact. And guess what? You can, too. Stay the course. Good Luck. Listen to my podcast.

Respectfully Submitted,

Neena R. Speer, Esq.

(Happiness, bar tutors, seeking self-awareness, and a heart for others are all key ingredients to making this young aspiring lawyer a complete and healthy person!)

My Journey as a Graduate

Graduation day is here… YOU did it! #WooHoo

Write about the tears you cried, the victory you feel, and the joy of being done. I'm so freaking proud of you!!!!!

_____

_____

_____

_____

_____

_____

_____

_____

_____

_____

_____

_____

_____

_____

_____

_____

The Bar Exam Diary

ent about the bar in any way you see fit. Write it out or draw it out. Just get it out of your own head and put something down here. It is a hard journey composed of many late nights, all-nighters, and early mornings, but I am a firm believer that you will pull though with a victory in the end. It took me two times to pass my bar exam, and it took some of my close friends and mentors of mine longer to pass theirs. I will always tell you this: YOU WILL PASS. And above all, once you pass, remember to stay humble because you have WORK LEFT TO DO.

Use this open space below to write out everything the bar exam puts you through, makes you feel, or forces you to think about…

Bar exam diary pt. 2 (continued)

Open space below…

Bar exam diary pt. 3 (continued)

Open space below...

Bar exam diary pt. 4 (continued)

Open space below…

Step 1-2-3 Mentor for Life Initiative

Info Sheet

Community service is more than just a line on a resume." This quote is one of the mottos Step 1-2-3: Mentor for Life Initiative bases our work on every day. The non-profit based out of Birmingham, AL is an organization working with students from kindergarten through college through mentorship in order to build a stronger and more cohesive community. More about our services can be found on YouTube under "Mentor for a Lifetime" search or our website step123mentor.org. On top of the L.A.S.T. Brand curated by Neena Speer, she is also the Founder of Step 1-2-3 Mentor for Life Initiative.

Highlights from the past two years include:

- A Hidden Figures Screening with NASA
- Invitation from The University of Alabama School of Law for Middle School Open House
- Speaker Series including guests from: Ken Perry Law Firm, Starbucks, NASA, The University of Alabama School of Law, Sleep Experts, our CEO, local lawyers, musicians, computer engineers, YMCA leaders, and more

- An Inaugural conference, #IAMLOST2018: How to Secure the Bag, for youth and adults. The conference focused on empowering those who were in their final steps of obtaining their degree or education and are unsure of the next step. The conference featured a keynote address from Chaucer Barnes, Chief Audience Officer at Translation LLC and United Masters, and testimonials featuring Kezia Williams, Herschell Hamilton, and Jessika Banks

- **Step 1-2-3 Virtual STEM Summer Camp i**s a virtual STEM summer camp provided for 6 FULL WEEKS. In response to COVID-19 and at our founding, Step 1-2-3 Mentor for Life Initiative has committed itself to provide safe and engaging alternatives to provide mentoring, education, and academic empowerment in virtual and in-person events, initiatives, and programs.

How You Can Help Now:

- **Mentor, Speak, or Partner:** Email us at Step123mentor@gmail.com if you see yourself impacting one life, speaking to our students about your career voluntarily, or being a partner on an upcoming event

- **Donate:** Cash App ($Step123Mentor); Crowdrise

- **Volunteer and Development:** Email us at step123mentor@gmail.com if you want to help implement our development initiatives and join a team of highly skilled leaders

- **Marketing and PR:** Send our emails to your networks, subscribe to our mailing lists through step123mentor.org

Book Neena as Your Next Speaker

Neena R. Speer, Esq.

Bio

From an early age, Speer's mother and father encouraged her that she was going to be a CEO.

Neena has since served as a YMCA summer camp counselor for over nine years and presently serves as the 2018 YMCA Birmingham's Give Campaign Face. Neena is a newly licensed attorney, a five-time published author for her Howard University honor's thesis and two University of Alabama School of Law papers, with one being published in the Harvard Journal on African American Public Policy. Neena is a proud African American and Indian mentor, speaker, and giver. Neena always tells her message with truth and authenticity.

As seen in:

The Black Girl Project ; National Pre-Law Diversity Conference ;

The University of Alabama School of Law ALABAMA LAW, etc.

Speaking Topics

The Importance of Diversity in Leadership Development

Diversity, it's an asset. Those who can't accept and respect other people may find it difficult to succeed in life and at work. Learn how to value others…

Founding a Non-Profit

When Neena began her Step 1-2-3 idea, she was eight years old, but it took until age 23 to make it happen. Learn the skills, plan, and contacts you must develop to make your dream happen…

Speak Your Truth Workshop: The LAST Brand: Lawyer, Author, Speaker, & Truth

Have you ever been LAST before? Well Neena has too. LAST picked on a team, LAST choice, and even LAST one to finish. Hear how she decided to change L.A.S.T. to a brand that is empowering…

"Always do the right things for the right reasons and you cannot go wrong. Stay disciplined and nothing you seek is beyond your reach."

--Neena's Family Mottos

Book NEENA SPEER for your next speaking event

NeenatheLASTbrand@gmail.com   **NeenatheLASTBrand.com**

IG Handle: @neena_rani
Podcast: Taking a Lunch with Neena

About the Author

Neena R. Speer, Esq.

Neena R. Speer is an attorney, author, speaker, and truth dealer. She has a solo law firm called the Neena R. Speer Law Firm LLC. She is a Founder and Executive Director of her mentoring nonprofit focused on continuous mentorship for all students at all levels K-12 & college, Step 1-2-3 Mentor for Life Initiative that she started her 3L year of law school. Lastly, she is a five-time published author with her most recent book is a republished Kindle version of Dear Future Lawyer: An Intimate Survival Guide for the Female Minority Law Student which hit #1 in two different categories in November 2020 earning her the title of Amazon Bestseller. Her passion since she was in eighth grade was to be a criminal defense attorney in her hometown where she grew up: Birmingham, AL. She is living out that dream and speaking for countless organizations including the University of Alabama School of Law, the YMCA, the Black Girl Project, the National HBCU Pre-Law Summit, Black Pre-Law Conference, Northern Illinois University Law School, various other organizations, and her upcoming TEDx Youth Davenport Talk entitled "Diversity Redefined" March 2021. She speaks about her experiences as a law student, a black minority in the law field, and her journey past failing her first bar exam. She specializes in Trademarks, Copyrights, Business Formation, Contracts Drafting/Review, Criminal Defense, and Family Law. a purpose driven, inspiring and dedicated professional, Neena Speer is a lawyer, a published writer, a CEO of her own non-profit & speaker. Also, she is the founder and executive director of the Step 1-2-3 Mentor for Life Initiative which is a non-profit geared towards developing lifelong mentors for students K-12 and college levels. Currently, Neena has written three published articles and has been asked to speak on various topics ranging from diversity and leadership, to the importance of integrity at the 2016 National Diversity Pre-Law Conference and Fair, at The University of Alabama School of Law as a presenter in 2017, a panelist in 2018, and at a recent 2018 Sisterhood Summit held in Brooklyn, NY. Neena has a BA (in French), a BS (in Psychology) from Howard University and a JD from The University of Alabama School of Law. Speer recently passed the Alabama Bar Exam and is excited to begin a career dedicated to helping impact her community one person, one step at a time.

Leave a Review

Hey Future Lawyers,

I see you made it to the end of my book. I hope that it was something of a phenomenal experience both writing in it and reading it. I want you to know how much it would mean to me to HEAR from you about your thoughts and feedback. I want you to know that I read ALL of my reviews.

Please leave a review online or email me at NeenatheLASTBrand@gmail.com for reviews on this book, the journal pages you want me to read, or testimonial videos that you want me to share on my social media outlets.

Thank you so much for reading my book. I hope it encouraged you, helped you take a real look at yourself, and inspired you. I look forward to hearing from you soon.

Sincerely,

Neena R. Speer, Esq.

Printed in the USA
CPSIA information can be obtained
at www.ICGtesting.com
LVHW050925111023
760608LV00027B/91

9 780692 163627